Collins

THE TRICK

KEITH GRAY

Illustrated by

Chapter 1

Eric's choice

A half-sucked sweet hit Eric White on the back of the head. It stuck in his hair. Everyone at the back of the bus burst out laughing. Two more sweets came flying Eric's way and he had to duck lower in his seat.

Mr Daniels was sitting at the front of the bus but he was on his feet in an instant. "Simmer down!" he bellowed. "If I've told you lot once, I've told you a thousand times. Best behaviour." The teacher glared at them. "All of you!"

Everyone went quiet. The kids on the back seat stared at their shoes or pretended to look out of the windows. But as soon as the teacher turned away and sat down again, Eric was pelted with a hail of sticky sweets. He pulled his coat over his head and tried to ignore it all.

It was cold and wet outside, the rain was pouring down, and the bus's windows had misted up inside. Eric used his finger to draw a big rectangle in the grey dampness of the window next to him. He made it look like a giant Ace of Spades. He didn't really care about the cold rain outside or the thrown sweets inside. He was feeling far too excited about where they were going.

He'd been looking forward to the trip for ages and had already made his mind up that nothing was going to spoil today.

Mr Daniels had run a competition for the whole class and the winner was allowed to choose where the class went on their end-of-term day trip. It had been a general knowledge quiz and Eric had been as surprised as anyone when he'd won. He'd thought long and hard about where he would choose for everyone to go.

Carter had told him that he should choose to go to a footy match. Carter said that if Eric didn't choose a footy match then he'd get a punch.

Penny Teller had told Eric he should choose to go shopping. She said she might be his girlfriend for a day if he did.

The trouble was, Eric didn't dream of playing for Man U or of owning a posh pair of shoes. And he knew most of the other kids called him a freak or a geek because what he really wanted was to be a magician.

Eric loved magic. Any time there was a magician on the TV, Eric watched it and recorded it. And then watched it again. He collected books that told you how to do card tricks. He'd even named his dog after his all-time favourite magician, Houdini.

It was almost by accident that Eric had spotted the poster in a newsagent's window:

But then it became very easy to choose where to go on the class trip.

The problem was no one else had been happy with Eric's choice. That was why he was sitting alone on the bus. It was why Penny Teller said she would never be his girlfriend, never in a million years. It was why he had a purple bruise on his arm where Carter had punched him.

But still, Eric couldn't help feeling excited about seeing a real magician live on stage.

Eric was drawing more pictures on the damp window when Carter suddenly sat down next to him. He was grinning and holding a pack of cards.

"I found your cards," Carter said.

Eric didn't even know his cards had gone missing. And he didn't trust Carter.

"You must have dropped them," Carter said.

"Or you stole them," Eric said.

Carter shrugged. "You want them or not?"

Eric took them and Carter hurried back down the bus to his mates on the back seat. They all started laughing again.

Eric always had some cards with him, so that he could show people a trick if they asked to see one. No one ever did ask, but Eric always carried his cards with him anyway, just in case.

He looked at Carter on the back seat. Carter grinned and waved. And his mates laughed even louder.

Last night Eric had stayed up late going over and over a new card trick he'd learned. Deep down he hoped he might meet Mathew Masters today, and maybe get to show him the new trick. But when Eric opened the pack he saw what everyone thought was so funny.

The Queen of Clubs had an eyepatch and a gap-toothed smile. The Jack of Diamonds had an arrow through his head. The King of Hearts was wearing a dress.

Every single card had been written or drawn on. They had rude pictures and swear words scrawled across them. All fifty-two cards. Ruined.

Chapter 2

The theatre

The theatre was huge and posh and massive and plush. Eric's class shuffled along the rows looking for their seats.

"Quietly now!" Mr Daniels bellowed. "No need to talk! You're not the only ones trying to enjoy yourselves."

Red curtains nearly as tall as Eric's house hid the stage. He would have loved to sit right on the front row, but Mr Daniels had already given them seat numbers and they had to sit where they were told. Eric was next to Penny Teller. He thought she was the prettiest girl in the class and usually he'd have been happy to sit next to her. But she was still complaining about Eric not choosing to go shopping.

"This is *boring*," she moaned.

"It's not started yet," Eric said.

"It doesn't need to *start*," she whined. "I already know it's *boring*."

So Eric ignored her.

He told himself it didn't matter what anyone else said or thought. This was going to be brilliant. Mathew Masters was a famous magician. Eric was going to see brand new tricks he'd never seen before. And he told himself to just be glad he was here at all, because this morning he'd been so late getting to school he'd almost missed the bus.

His mum had made him look after his baby sister, Lottie, while she had breakfast. He'd also had to feed Lottie while his mum took a shower.

Then his mum had spent so long fighting with Lottie's dad on the phone that Eric had had to change Lottie's nappy twice. He often thought it was one of the most amazing tricks the way Lottie made so much stuff magically appear in her nappy.

When his mum had at last finished on the phone, she'd asked Eric to go to the shops for her. But he'd pretended he hadn't heard her as he'd grabbed his bag and run out of the door.

He'd run all the way to school, getting soaking wet and out of breath, and had only just been in time to catch the bus to the theatre.

The big problem was he knew he would be in deep trouble when he got home again tonight. Not for running off when his mum wanted him to do the shopping, but because he'd left the front door open in his hurry and the dog had got out.

His mum had sent him an angry text:

Houdini's escaped!!!

The angrier his mum was, the more exclamation marks she used. Three was really bad news.

Sitting in the theatre, Eric pushed his worries to the back of his mind. He stared at the massive red curtains in front of the stage and let himself get excited all over again.

"Why are you into this stuff?" Penny Teller asked. "It's not like it's *real*, you know."

Of course Eric knew magic wasn't real. "It would be brilliant if it *was* real, wouldn't it?" he said.

"But it's *not*," Penny said.

Eric shrugged.

Penny pointed at his sleeve. "What's that on your jumper?" she asked. "That stuff. *Yuk*. What is it?"

Eric blushed and pushed his sleeve up to hide the stain. "Curry sauce," he lied, thinking of Lottie's two magic nappy tricks that morning.

Luckily, he didn't have to say any more because the lights started to dim. Mr Daniels bellowed at everyone to be quiet. And the huge curtains opened.

Chapter 3

The magician

Eric sat there goggle-eyed and grinning as the magician performed. He was enjoying himself so much he forgot all about the bad stuff that had happened earlier. Mathew Masters maybe looked a bit old-fashioned wearing a top hat and a jacket with long tails at the back, but Eric thought he was the best magician he'd ever seen.

Mathew Masters made a skeleton dance.

He made £100 appear inside a solid block of ice.

He made a rabbit fly.

Eric was happy to see Penny Teller clapping and laughing as much as he was. She didn't seem bored any more. And Eric even saw Carter looking amazed when Mathew Masters did his best trick.

The magician wheeled what looked like a tall black wardrobe into the middle of the stage. It had swirls and licks of silver and gold fire painted on the sides. Eric had seen plenty of magic cabinets before and tried to guess what was going to happen next.

Mathew Masters spun the cabinet around on its wheels to show there were no secret doors at the back or sides. He turned it so everyone in the audience could see all the way inside. Then he threw in a whole deck of playing cards, one after the other, very quickly. Every card vanished instantly.

He took his top hat off and threw that in too.

Gone.

In the blink of an eye.

Eric was totally impressed. When other magicians put things inside a magic cabinet, they had to close the door before they could make them vanish. This magic cabinet didn't even have a door. Anything Mathew Masters put inside disappeared into thin air. Even flying rabbits.

The magician bowed deeply and waited for the clapping to quieten down. Then he stepped up to the front of the stage.

"A pack of cards was easy," he said. "My hat and the rabbit? Nothing could be simpler. But what about a person? Can this incredible cabinet make a person vanish?" He smiled at the audience. "I need a volunteer. Who should I make disappear?"

It took Carter maybe as long as half a second to shout, "Eric! Make Eric disappear!"

And then the rest of class joined in. "Eric! Er-ric!"

"Where are you, Eric?" Mathew Masters called. "Come up on stage and join me."

Eric was nervous but excited, too. He was going to be part of a magic trick, on stage, for real. He wondered if he should take his pack of cards with him. But then he remembered what Carter and his mates had done to them.

"Hurry up, lad!" Mr Daniels bellowed. "Don't keep Mr Masters waiting."

Eric squeezed along the row of seats, bumping knees and stepping on feet. He walked towards the stage. Yes, he was nervous, but he was also beaming a big, massive, face-splitting grin.

Carter shouted, "Disappear, and don't come back!"

Even when everybody laughed, Eric couldn't stop grinning.

He went up the steps to the stage and blinked in the bright lights. He couldn't see his class because the lights were shining right in his face, but he could still hear them chanting his name. He shook hands with Mathew Masters and the magician winked at him.

"Eric, are you ready to travel to a place you've never been before?" Mathew Masters asked, loud enough for the whole audience to hear. "Are you ready to do something truly magical? Are you ready, Eric, to vanish – not *somewhere*, but *Elsewhere*?"

Eric nodded. His heart was beating fast. "I think so."

"Then dare to walk into my magic cabinet," Mathew Masters boomed, pointing at the empty black space.

The cabinet was bigger on the inside, more like a corridor than a box. And pitch black. Eric held his hands out in front of himself as he walked forward.

"And mind the step," the magician whispered, so only Eric could hear.

Chapter 4

Behind the cabinet

There was a hidden door at the back of the cabinet. Eric pushed it open and stepped through.

He stepped into a dimly-lit room. The door slammed shut behind him, making him jump. He almost kicked a rabbit. It ran away from under his foot, hopping and skidding across the wooden floor. It had to dodge playing cards and silk scarves as it ran. It hopped inside the magician's top hat, which was on the floor under a chair.

Eric needed a moment to let his head sort out what his eyes were seeing. How on earth could this big room be behind that little cabinet on the stage? He reckoned he just wasn't clever enough to work it out yet. It was all part of the trick.

The room was long and thin. It smelled of damp and cigar smoke. Eric counted thirteen dark doors around the room, including the one he'd come through. He wondered where they all led.

The walls were covered in posters for famous magicians from history. Eric had read about some of them: David Devant, Harry Kellar, John Henry Pepper and Eric's favourite, Harry Houdini. There was a sagging armchair covered with moons and stars next to Eric's door and he sat down to see what would happen next.

Then he realised he wasn't alone in the room. A young woman reading a magazine sat opposite. She glanced up at him and smiled. She was wearing a red bow tie and a top hat covered in fake jewels. Eric smiled back, his smile a bit lop-sided.

"Are you a magician?" he asked.

"I'm a magical assistant," she told him. "I'm Barbara."

"I'd love to be a magician," Eric said.

"So what's stopping you?" she asked.

He shrugged. He'd never been asked that before. When he'd told his mum he wanted to be a magician, she'd said he should grow up, get his head out of the clouds, think about a proper job. And the kids at school just laughed.

A sudden flapping at Eric's ear startled him. He leapt to his feet, hands in the air, fighting off …

Fighting off a fluttering white dove. He blushed, knowing Barbara was watching.

The dove circled the room once, then sank to the floor where it strutted and pecked amongst all the cards.

"You shouldn't be too long," Barbara said. "Just wait for your door to open again."

Eric nodded. Then, just to be sure, he asked, "That one? The one I came in through?"

"Oh yes," she said. "All sorts of trouble if you go back through a different door." She raised her eyebrows. "Been there, done that. Big fuss."

Eric put his ear to the door he'd come through. He couldn't hear anything on the other side. He couldn't hear anyone clapping, or Carter shouting, or Mr Daniels bellowing.

He told himself he didn't need to feel nervous. It was all just a trick. Yet Eric couldn't help thinking that this room felt *weird*. Really weird. He thought he'd seen weird things before, but this room was even weirder than Lady Gaga or vegan sausages.

Chapter 5

The escape artist

Something crashed. Something rattled. And a door further along the room burst open. A man wrapped in chains and padlocks, with a sack over his head, tumbled into the room, rolling across the floor. Eric ran to help the man, who bucked and thrashed, rattled and clattered.

"It's okay, leave him," Barbara said.

"But …" Eric said. "But …"

A tall, thickly tanned woman wearing a sparkly cat suit and a feather headdress followed through the same door. "I'm coming. I'm here. Stop fussing. Sheila's here."

She knelt on the man's back, plucked a key from her headdress and undid the padlocks one at a time. The man threw off the chains. His fingers grabbed at the sack's drawstring and he yanked it off his head. He gasped. His slick-black hair was ruffled, his cheeks sweaty-red.

"Good grief. Did you see how tight that fellow tied this thing?" He rubbed at his neck, at the bright line of rope burn. "They're a tough audience to please tonight, wouldn't you say?"

"They've paid a lot to see you," Sheila said.

"Yes, yes, they have," the escape artist said. "And, by Jove, I'll give them a show to remember!" He had a booming voice, like an excited headmaster.

"Their applause will be loud enough to rock the whole ship," he continued. "We'll make the ocean swell on waves of applause. We'll make the very sea crash with the sound …"

"Yes, yes," Sheila said. "If you say so." She turned to Barbara and rolled her eyes. But she smiled as she did so. "And how are you, Barbara? Things okay with you, love?"

"Good, thanks," Barbara said, returning the smile. "Really great audience tonight. The applause hasn't stopped."

Eric was listening to everything they were saying. He reckoned it must feel good to hear applause so often. It wasn't like he wanted his mum to clap every time he changed Lottie's nappy. But a thank you now and again would definitely be nice.

Sheila turned to Eric. "And who is it you're seeing, love?"

Eric wasn't sure what she meant. "Hmm?"

"Whose show are you at?"

"Oh," he said. "Mathew Masters."

Sheila seemed very happy about that. "Young Matty still on the go, is he? That's good to know. Which theatre is that, then?"

Eric thought it was a strange question. "The one in town," he said. Because there was only one theatre in town.

Sheila looked suddenly awkward. "Right, of course. Yes." She nodded quickly and her headdress spilled a pink feather. "That theatre in town. Of course it is."

Eric watched the pink feather float to the floor and wondered where the escape artist and his assistant had come from. Was there a second magic show on at the theatre? Surely he would have heard about it.

He looked at the door they'd come through. Where did that door go?

Chapter 6

Abraca-Barbara

"Right," Sheila said to the escape artist. "Our audience will be thinking you've fallen overboard. Time to get back and wow them." She combed her fingers through his hair, slicking it back for him.

The escape artist flung the chains over his shoulder, puffed out his chest. "And wow them we will! We'll amaze them! We'll astonish them! We'll …"

"Yes, yes," Sheila said. "You've told me that already." She shoved him through the door, back the way they'd come. "Cheerio, Barbara," she called. "And enjoy your show," she said to Eric.

The door closed behind them.

Eric watched them go. But he had no idea where to. The gears in his head weren't quite meshing.

Barbara was looking at him closely. "Everything okay?"

He shrugged. "Are you waiting to reappear, too?"

"No. It's transformation night for me tonight." She hooked a thumb at the door behind her. "A pig's going to come running through there. That's my cue to leap out on stage. And, *alacazam*! I was a snorting pig, but now I'm a girl in a daft hat with sparkly bits."

"A pig?"

She nodded.

"My stage name is Abraca-Barbara."

"I didn't know there were two magicians doing shows," Eric said. "Three, I mean." He pointed at the door Sheila and the escape artist had used.

"Our shows aren't on at your theatre," Barbara said.

Eric pretended this made sense. "There's not another theatre next door, is there? I thought it was a kebab house." He looked at the thirteen doors around the room. "This is backstage, right?"

"Well … sort of."

Eric pointed at the escape artist's door. "They were talking about ships. Cruise ships?"

"Yes."

"But you don't get cruises in town."

"No."

Eric stood up, in case that helped him think. "I walked through a door at the back of the cabinet, right? And ended up here, backstage? But the audience thinks I've disappeared?"

Barbara nodded. "Yes."

"But how can here be backstage to lots of different places?" He scratched the back of his neck, at the chilly spot at the top of his spine that he'd just this second noticed.

Abraca-Barbara said, "Don't worry. Your theatre's back through that door you came in. As soon as it opens, you go through, and *pop* you're back again."

Eric thought about this. He pointed at the door behind her. "So where does that one go?"

"Barcelona."

"*Barcelona*?"

Chapter 7

Elsewhere

Eric slumped back into the armchair. His head was a mad mess of confusion. Something prodded at his spine. He pulled a long wand from down the back of the armchair's cushion. A very long wand. He pulled hand over hand. Very, *very* long. He gave up and let it stick out above his head at an odd angle.

Barbara came over and knelt beside him. "Where did you think people went when they disappeared?"

"Nowhere. I thought it was just a trick."

"This is nowhere, and somewhere," Barbara said. "It's hard to explain. But think of it as another *where*. It was created by some of the world's greatest magicians and linked to thirteen magical cabinets."

She pointed at the antique posters around the room. "Devant, Kellar, Houdini."

"Houdini?" Eric's ears pricked up. "He's been here?"

Barbara nodded. "Brilliant magic men and women. Of course, small-fry magicians use fake panels, or mirrors, even computers these days. They're the ones doing *tricks*. But this is a great tradition. Thirteen magical cabinets passed down from magician to magician that really can make people and things disappear to *another-where*. We call it *Elsewhere*."

Eric had always kind of hoped, dreamed, that magic might be true, but …

He strode over to the escape artist's door. Ignoring Barbara's warning, he yanked it open.

An audience of orange and wrinkly old people in shorts and sunhats, holding iced drinks with paper umbrellas, stared back at him. They swayed one way, then the other. Sheila was being sawn in half. Eric had time to hear a seagull call before the door slammed shut.

He blinked. Twice. He thought he'd smelled coconuts.

Barbara put a hand on his shoulder. "Gets us all a bit funny first time."

"But it's impossible," Eric said.

"Yes," Barbara agreed. "That's why it's magic."

Before Barbara could stop him, he pulled open another door. A man wearing a turban was climbing a long rope that went up into the sky. He waved at Eric.

Barbara put a hand on Eric's shoulder and pushed the door closed. She led him back to the armchair next to his door.

"But why don't I know about it?" he asked. "I love magic. Why doesn't the whole world know?"

"They do. They just don't believe."

"So how did you get here?"

"Same as you," she said. "It gets boring being in the audience all the time, doesn't it? Sometimes you want to be part of the show and see what it's like being on the stage for a while."

Before Eric could ask anything else, Barbara's door burst open and a pig in a sparkly top hat and bow tie charged into the room. Its trotters slid on the wooden floor, sending up a swirl of cards and glitter and silk scarves.

"That's mc," Barbara said. "Nice to meet you, Eric. Enjoy the rest of your show."

"People are going to think I'm mad if I tell them about this." He could imagine the look on his mum's face and hear the abuse from Carter and Penny Teller.

"So don't tell them."

Eric nodded. She was right. This was a big, huge, massive secret. He didn't have to tell anyone if he didn't want to.

"Mathew must be building up to an impressive reappearance for you," Barbara said. "He's kept you here long enough to be the big ending of his whole show. Think of the applause when you step out of that cabinet."

She winked. "Gotta love that applause."

Abraca-Barbara stepped through her door. Eric heard a split-second of cheers before it closed behind her.

He untangled a silk scarf from the pig's back legs and the pig oinked in a very real way. He didn't think he was clever enough to imagine such a realistic oink. And he liked having a secret. He liked knowing something hardly anybody else knew. He liked knowing how the trick really worked.

The door back to Mathew Masters's magic cabinet on the stage in the theatre in town swung open. Carter, Penny Teller and bellowing Mr Daniels were all back through that door. Back there was a missing dog, an angry mother and a baby sister who filled her nappy quicker than Eric could fill her bottle.

He doubted it was raining in Barcelona.

He remembered the smell of coconuts and wondered where the cruise ship was heading.

He turned to look at the other doors around the room. Then picked one, any one.

He stood in front of it. He put his ear to it. But there was only one way to find out which stage and how much applause was waiting beyond.

He took a breath and reached for the handle.

Reader challenge

Word hunt

 On page 2, find a verb that means "shouted".

2 On page 26, find a verb that means "to avoid".

3 On page 46, find an adjective that means "very old".

Story sense

 Why did Eric get teased about liking magic?

5 How did Eric feel when Mathew Masters asked him to go up on the stage? (pages 21 and 22)

6 Why was Eric confused when the escape artist and Sheila talked about a ship and other theatres? (pages 35–36)

7 Why did Eric have a "chilly spot at the top of his spine"? (page 43)

 Why do you think Eric decided to go through a different door at the end? (page 52)

Your views

9 Did you think the author made "Elsewhere" sound realistic? Give reasons.

10 If you were Eric, what would you have done at the end of the story? Give reasons.

Spell it

With a partner, look at these words and then cover them up.

- appear
- disappear
- reappear

Take it in turns for one of you to read the words aloud. The other person has to try and spell each word. Check your answers, then swap over.

Try it

With a partner, discuss what you think was behind the door that Eric went through in the end. Take it in turns to write three sentences each to describe what he saw when he went through the door.

William Collins's dream of knowledge for all began with the publication of his first book in 1819. A self-educated mill worker, he not only enriched millions of lives, but also founded a flourishing publishing house. Today, staying true to this spirit, Collins books are packed with inspiration, innovation and practical expertise. They place you at the centre of a world of possibility and give you exactly what you need to explore it.

Collins. Freedom to teach.

Published by Collins Education
An imprint of HarperCollins*Publishers*
77–85 Fulham Palace Road
Hammersmith
London
W6 8JB

Browse the complete Collins Education catalogue at **www.collinseducation.com**

Text © Keith Gray 2012
Illustrations © Chris Coady 2012

Series consultants: Alan Gibbons and Natalie Packer

10 9 8 7 6 5 4 3 2 1
ISBN 978-0-00-746490-6

British Library Cataloguing in Publication Data.
A catalogue record for this publication is available from the British Library.

Commissioned by Catherine Martin
Edited and project-managed by Sue Chapple
Illustration management by Tim Satterthwaite
Proofread by Grace Glendinning
Design and typesetting by Jordan Publishing Design Limited
Cover design by Paul Manning

Acknowledgements

The publishers would like to thank the students and teachers of the following schools for their help in trialling the Read On series:

Southfields Academy, London
Queensbury School, Queensbury, Bradford
Langham C of E Primary School, Langham, Rutland
Ratton School, Eastbourne, East Sussex
Northfleet School for Girls, North Fleet, Kent
Westergate Community School, Chichester, West Sussex
Bottesford C of E Primary School, Bottesford, Nottinghamshire
Woodfield Academy, Redditch, Worcestershire
St Richard's Catholic College, Bexhill, East Sussex